# ROSIE'S WALK

# Pat Hutchins

# ROSIE'S WALK

Simon & Schuster Books for Young Readers

SIMON & SCHUSTER BOOKS FOR YOUNG READERS
An imprint of Simon & Schuster Children's Publishing Division
1230 Avenue of the Americas
New York, New York 10020
Copyright © 1968 by Patricia Hutchins
All rights reserved including the right of reproduction
in whole or in part in any form.

Simon & Schuster Books for Young Readers is a trademark of Simon & Schuster

44 46 48 50 49 47 45

Library of Congress catalog card number 68-12090
ISBN 978-0-02-745850-3
Manufactured in China
0419 SCP

For
Wendy
and
Stephen

Rosie the hen went for a walk

# across the yard

around
the
pond

over the haystack

past the mill

through the fence

# under the beehives

and
got back
in time
for dinner.

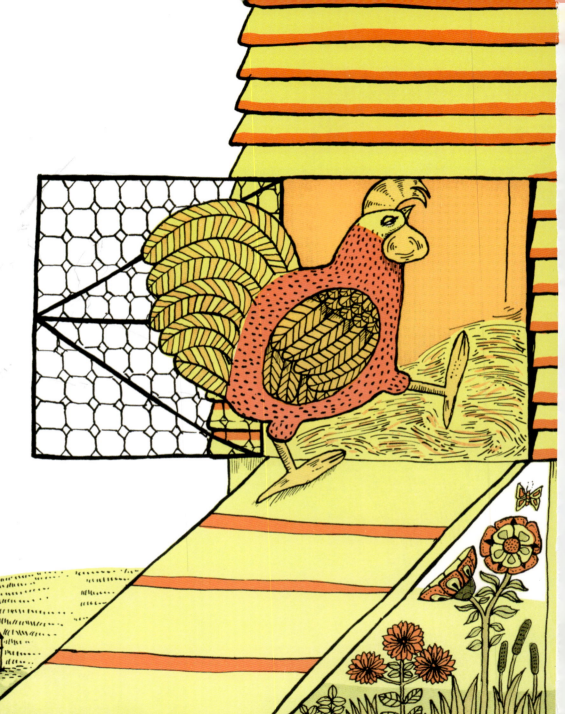